K.A. Appleby wrote *The Source* whilst on a family vacation to Murcia. She has worked for Barclays Bank UK for the last 13 years and writes as a hobby in her spare time. She is married to Glenn, has two grown-up children, Chloe and Thomas, and lives in Houghton le Spring. She is an avid crime fiction reader. It is her love of reading that inspired her to write her debut short story, *The Source*.

GW00585222

This book is dedicated firstly to my husband, for having patience with me to complete it, believing in me and supporting me. My children, Chloe and Thomas. My mother, Julie, my father, Paul, step father, Martin, sisters; Marie, Lyndsey, Naomi, Megan and my brother Andrew. All equally precious to me.

K.A. Appleby

THE SOURCE

AUSTIN MACAULEY PUBLISHERS™

LONDON · CAMBRIDGE · NEW YORK · SHARJAH

A CIP catalogue record for this title is available from the British Library.

ISBN 9781788788373 (Paperback)
ISBN 9781528914055 (ePub e-book)

www.austinmacauley.com

First Published 2022
Austin Macauley Publishers Ltd®
1 Canada Square
Canary Wharf
London
E14 5AA

I would like to thank Austin Macauley Publishers for taking a chance on me and believing in my work. Without them and their ongoing support, this wouldn't be possible.

A jealous girlfriend is a faithful. If she doesn't get jealous when someone has your attention, it's because someone has hers.

Part 1

Chapter 1
Linda, 1952

Susan had always been cleverer than Linda. She knew it too; always at the top of the class, at the top of the cheerleaders, top scorer in maths and even geeky science. She was the most popular girl in school, she always had a boyfriend and, much to Linda's hatred, she was constantly living in her twin sister's shadow.

They were born 3 Min 20 seconds apart, with Susan being the oldest. They were born to Nancy and Teddy. After many years of trying for a baby, Nancy and Teddy were eventually blessed with two beautiful daughters. They had a normal upbringing, their father being a police officer and their mother a housewife, they were always kept on the right side of the law. Teddy wouldn't stand for any nonsense and expected Linda and Susan to be in for family dinner when he arrived back from a long day at the station. He would tell the girls awful stories of murders and talk about the latest 'no marks', with Nancy telling him to stop it. It was at one of the family dinners that he mentioned a recent 'no mark' JIMMY JENKINS that got Susan blushing. Susan was good at pulling the wool over Nancy and Teddy's eyes but not Linda.

Linda was actually pleased there was one thing she was better at doing than her sister was, recognising when someone was lying; that night as the girls headed up to bed, she sang: JIMMY JIMMY WHERE FOR ART THOU JIMMY! Just as Linda got to the top stair, she felt a fist in her face…it was Susan.

"Bitch, stop singing that you don't know who he is nor do I, so shut it, I mean it…I'll hit you again, I'll tell Mam and Dad you fell on the stair, they know how clumsy you are, Linda!"

Without a fight, Linda retreated to her room. They may be twins, but they certainly didn't share anything; toys, friends, clothes, not even looks. They were both unique in their own ways. Linda knew she'd hit a nerve; lying in bed, she decided when the time was right, she would catch Susan out…and by god she did!

Chapter 2
Jimmy, 1952

Jimmy couldn't believe his luck; a nice little blonde, ten years his junior, had just left his bed, and he was well happy. He was in a good place now. He had the face of an angel but the temper of a mad man. His looks were what got him into trouble these days although it was also a magnet for the ladies, so in that sense, he didn't mind. Looking around him, he was proud of who he was and what he had achieved. He was a looker. Jimmy, with his brown hair slicked back into his teddy boy quiff and his big blue eyes, was a ladies' man, and he knew it. You see Jimmy could have any girl he wanted.

But this girl was different. He needed to keep her sweet, her old man's a copper and he needs info, or he's a goner.

Jimmy looked at his Rolex. "Shit! I am late," Dressing quickly with the suit, he paid cash for yesterday. He gently brushed the blue wool suit with pride. As he looked in the mirror, he caught sight of his left cheek and flinched. The scar was fading but still visible to him.

"Right, Jimmy, boy let's get your arse down to the club," he said.

Chapter 3
Linda

Linda knew she'd seen Susan get into a pink Mustang right outside of the school gates. She knew if she told Dad, it would stop Susan in her tracks, but she'd caught a glimpse of this Jimmy as he held the door for Susan, and shameful to say it. She thought he was a good-looking boy! It was then she noticed a blue Cortina following the Mustang. She was on her bike quick as a flash, being in the last grade at school and almost 16. They were allowed to take their bikes as a treat. Linda's heart was racing as she sped behind the Cortina. She was struggling to keep up, and with her asthma, this wasn't such a good idea. She was sweating and panting; she was struggling to breathe; she stopped, put her hand into her rucksack and pulled her blue inhaler out and gently breathed in. After a few moments, her breathing had started to regain normality, and it was just then the Cortina stopped and reversed alongside Linda.

Ah God, thought Linda, *what do I do?*

The window of the driver's side wound down and, to Linda's amazement, a woman with striking green eyes and luscious blonde curly hair spoke to her.

"Hi, I was tailgating that Mustang up in front, and I saw you in my rear view; you didn't seem right. Are you OK?"

The lady spoke in such a mesmerising soft voice that Linda was in a daze; she was captivated by the sheer beauty of this stranger.

"Excuse me, lady, are you OK? Can you hear me?"

"Sorry, yeah I'm fine thanks av. Just got asthma; I had an attack, but am OK now, thanks."

"Well, can I give you a lift home, maybe just to make sure you're safe?" Linda thought about how hard it would be to pedal all the way back to her place and reluctantly accepted the lift. She jumped in with her bike on the back seat and proceeded to give directions.

"Let's do some introductions; what's your name, beautiful?"

"I'm Linda, so what's your name?"

"I'm Patricia; Pat for short, always hated the name."

Linda thought about the next question carefully; she didn't want to get Susan into trouble.

"So, Pat, can I ask why you were tailing that car? Are you a copper?"

Pat laughed. "No Darlin' I'm not; I'm doing a bit of business for a friend."

"What sort of business? Just this and that? Is it to do with Jimmy?"

"What do you know about Jimmy, love? How do you know him?"

Linda was backtracking; now she was frightened.

"Did I say 'Jimmy', sorry a meant to say 'Jim'. I…er…my dad's a copper; he'll be worried about me; please, can we just get home…please?" Pat stared a long deep hard stare at Linda.

What did she know about her Jimmy, and who was in that car with him? She had to be careful she wasn't about to expose who she was to a kid, let alone a kid whose dad was a copper.

"OK, love, no problem." They didn't speak for the rest of the 25-minute journey home until they pulled up outside and Pat spoke first, "There you go, Linda, home safe and sound."

"Thanks, Pat; thanks for the lift. I appreciate it really, I do see you around, kid." It wasn't until Pat was out of sight that Linda realised her bike was still on the back seat.

"Shit! What would Mam and Dad say?" She closed the door behind her and made her way to the dinner table where, to her amazement, Susan was sitting, wolfing her shepherd's pie.

Chapter 4
Pat

"Answer the bloody phone, Jimmy…" She hated it when Jimmy ignored her, but they'd been together over 12 months now, and they were like chalk and cheese. His looks and demure were what attracted Pat to him. She lit a cigarette and inhaled, slowly gathering her thoughts. She would always stand by her Jimmy no matter how many floozies took his fancy. Like Jimmy said this floozie was different, they needed her for info on what was going down on RON SIDMONDS club, her dad being responsible for arresting him and shutting the club down. Pat smiled; the plan was coming together. One thing was missing; they needed to know where the cash was, but all Pat had to do was to pay her old boyfriend Ron a visit at HM Prison Durham and flutter her eyelashes to gain his trust again. For sure, he would tell her where he hid the cash, and then she and Jimmy would be free to get their one-way ticket to Los Alcázares to start a new life. She knew exactly what her next steps were although she didn't like the fact of Jimmy sleeping with that girl Susan one bit. She decided she would keep a closer eye on Jimmy and that would start tonight at the club.

Pat arrived at the club just off Granger Street at 10 p.m. She'd always hated the name her dad had given the club: GUYS AND DOLLS. When her dad died, and she and her brother Davey took over the club, she made a promise she wouldn't change the name out of respect for her father, but she still loathed the name. She pulled her fur coat into her neck; it was cold tonight—a definite chill in the air. She hurried through the club's side entrance, expecting to find Jimmy waiting for her as usual.

Just then Davey, her brother, shouted over to her, "Hey Pat! There's a message for ya. Jimmy had to go out and do a bit business. He said he be going straight home and he'll call you in the mornin'; you done summit wrong, love?" Pat's eyes saw red; he never did this to her; he always met her at the club at 10 every Friday and Saturday night, so what had changed?

"No, a bloody haven't you, cheeky sod; like you said he's got some business to attend to and actually so have I. Can you look after things here on ay own Davey tonight?"

"Yeah, no probs, Pat love, you can count on me, a might even get the boys down for a bit of poker out the back eh?"

"Do what you like, Davey; it's your club as well." Pat wasn't interested one bit what Davey was planning; her thoughts were entirely on where her Jimmy was, and more to the question who with.

Chapter 5
Teddy

Teddy had just started his shift down at the cop shop. In the twenty years he'd worked here, he'd seen it decorated once, and that was when he had a women governor only because she couldn't stand the colour on the walls of the lads smokes. She said it had turned the walls morello brown!

God! twenty years, where's the time gone, he thought, *this place is as drab as ever.* Dropping to bits like the rest of the force, he was sure if he could crack this big case with the governor's job up for grabs, he was sure to be recommended by the guv. The way he saw was he's put away a list of wrong'uns as long as your arm, but no one had managed to arrest Ron; mind you, it took him ten years of trying, and finally, he got him. Teddy snapped out of his daydream when he was summoned into the governor's office.

"DCI Cartwright, can I have a word, in my office shut the door behind you. take a seat, teddy…a scotch?"

"Is there a problem, guv? Or is it your retirement do? I'm on the ball; it's all in hand. We got another four months to…"

The governor wasn't happy; he stopped Teddy in his tracks; he would have to tactfully break the news to his oldest friend, and it wasn't going to be easy.

"Look, Teddy, I'm not going to beat about the bush; there's no easy way of saying this, but we've been tailing JIMMY JENKINS, and my sources tell me your daughter Susan left his flat last night at 11:30. Now, Teddy, I know this is not what you want to hear, but you have to believe this. Your girl is mixed up with this Jimmy. She can't be involved in this case. We can't afford to screw this operation up, Teddy, do you hear me, lad?"

"You got it wrong, sir, my Susan is a good girl; Jimmy Jenkins? He's a good ten years older than my Susan."

"Look! I suggest you get yourself off home, Ted; it's near midnight. Please don't let her know that we know she was with him. We can't afford any setbacks, and we don't know whether he's using her for information. Let me think we need to get this right. I'll call you tonight to let you know how we proceed. DCI Blue Water is tailing Jimmy for now, and it stays that way. I don't want you anywhere near, Teddy, do you hear me?"

Teddy could hear the guv load and clear. His mind was thinking all sorts. His heart was racing. Not his sweet innocent Susan; she's not mixed up with him, she can't be…he knew he had to obey the guv.

"Am off now, guv, I shall expect your call this evening." Teddy grabbed his hat and coat and made his way out of the station; he knew where he was going, and it wasn't home. He was headed straight to the 'Hoarse and Hound' on Granger Street to get rat-arsed.

Chapter 6
Pat

Pat was livid; she'd seen with her own eyes Susan leave Jimmy's flat. Why was she jealous? After all, it was her idea. She was the one who begged Jimmy to seduce Susan. She hadn't thought the plan through; Susan was ten years younger than her, she had a better figure than Pat, and her eyes were piercing blue. Her waist-length hair was thick and blonde, her legs to die for.

"Oh, Jimmy!" The tears came fast. Why had she settled for this life? What if Jimmy left her for this kid? He was lying to her, and he had never lied to her in the past. Something had changed. Susan changed his way of thinking. Pat looked at her watch again; 12:30. She'd been sat since she saw Susan leave. What was she going to do next? She needed to act fast; that's when she remembered Linda's bike.

"Bingo! I'll pay the Cartwrights a little visit tomorrow." But first, she had debts to collect from THE 'Hoarse and Hound'.

As she walked into the club, she glanced at the bar. "This place is fucking going down the pan, never any fucker in these days." She scanned the club until she found the owner. "Timmy, you got my rent?"

"Not quite, Pat; just give me a few more hours; I'll have all of it, av. Got DCI Cartwright drinking like there's no tomorrow. He's rat-arsed in the back; he's already spent a ton. He's been gambling and ranting about how he's gonna be guvner soon; he's lost a wad."

"Where did you say he was? Out the back?"

"Yeah, been in an hour and a half at least. He can't even walk straight, Pat, there's summit up with him. I'll put my life on it; he's not his usual miserable self."

Pat walked out the back and slid beside Teddy. He wasn't bad-looking for his age; he was rugged and a bit edgy even for a copper. His black hair centred had a car flick, and she could see he was clearly unshaven. He stunk of booze and wasn't aware she was sitting beside him. It was then and their Pat decided she wanted to know more about Teddy Cartwright.

Chapter 7
Jimmy

Jimmy was heading down to the club. He'd tried ringing Pat as promised. No answer. He looked around him; soon he'd be far, far away from here; just him and Susan; away from Pat, and there's nothing no one could do about it. Jimmy was falling for Susan. He knew she was younger, but he loved it; she made him smile, and he thought he may even go on the straight and narrow for this girl. How he would break it to Pat would be the hard one. She wasn't to know until he's out of the country. He was daydreaming what life with Susan would be like; sipping cocktails and lying in the sun in a beautiful villa in Rio. Just then the phone rang.

"Jimmy, it's Tim from the 'Hoarse and Hound'. Can you come and get Pat? She's been here all night. She's had a right old drink; she's been cosying up to that DCI Cartwright. They were laughing and joking, Jimmy. I swear I told Pat I'll tell ay; she couldn't care less. You best get down quick." Jimmy slammed the receiver off the wall. How dare she? Make a mock of him? He was boss; she did what he said. He clenched his fist. It had been a while, but Pat would know what was coming to her…

Barging through the club, Jimmy was like a mad man. "Where is she, Tim? You fucking tell me now where is she?"

"She's upstairs, sleeping it off. Please keep it down eh, Jim, my punters are watching."

"I'll do what the fuck I want; you listening, now piss off."

He ran up the stairs. Pat had heard everything. She locked the door from the inside. She'd seen his fury many times before and knew what to expect. She was trembling with fear, but she also knew if she didn't open up, he would kill her for sure.

"Open up, Pat, I swear to God if you've told that DCI anything with that runaway mouth of yours, I'll kill ay. OPEN UP NOW!"

Pat unlocked the door. Jimmy charged for the door knocking her sideways as he kicked it open. He lunged for Pat. He grabbed her by the hair and flung her across the room. She cowered in the corner, waiting for the next blow. It came hard across her face. She knew she was bleeding. She felt something warm trickle down her face. She knew he kept a knuckle duster on him, and the force of the blow, he had no doubt used it. It was best not to say anything during the attacks. She'd learned that from day one. She was waiting for Jimmy's rage to subside before picking herself up off the floor and making her way into the bathroom. He followed her and spoke softly as if nothing had happened. It was a pattern, you see; he would be remorseful after and say he would never do it again and she believed him.

"Clean yourself up, love; there's a good girl, and meet me at the club at 7, I'll let myself out."

She looked in the mirror and screamed, "YOU BASTARD JIMMY!"

Chapter 8
Susan

"Look, Jimmy, Linda knows about us. I'm worried Dad will find out. I don't want you going back inside because of me. I think we need to cool it for a while. I'm sorry, Jimmy."

Susan placed the receiver down quietly. She'd just left Jimmy a message that she knew he wouldn't be happy about although it was all part of the plan. She decided there and then she wasn't giving up on them; not at all. She was just buying them time.

She dreamed of their new life, just the two of them, just the way Jimmy had described. She knew what she had to do. They'd spoken about it often enough, and it wasn't going to be easy, betraying her father. She decided it would do little harm to take a sneak peek at the case files on RON and decide what to do with the information from there. She opened the office door. She hesitated…the drawer was locked! Of course, it would be, how stupid of her! Just then she heard the front door…

"Susan, are you home?" It was Linda.

"Yeah, I'm upstairs. av just been to the loo. I thought you were at dance practice?"

"Susan, you should have seen me doing the lindy hop! That's my fav now; just wish I had a good-looking boy like you to dance with all night!"

Susan was livid; all the remarks Linda kept making she should just come out and say that she knows she was fed up!

"Yea, you mean my Jimmy, Linda? The 'no mark' as Dad calls him?"

"Yes, Susan, actually that is the one; ten years your senior n all, with a Mrs as well, aww, didn't you know about her?"

"Of course, I know about her. He's leaving her anyway. We are running away together, and there's nothing no one can do about it, and if you so much as tell Dad about this, I'll have you. Now shut up, Linda, and leave me alone."

Running into the bedroom, her eyes were full. She was in love with him. She'd really fallen for him. She needed to know for sure if he felt the same way. She knew he did, but when he asked her to get some info on Ron, she wasn't too sure. Jimmy had told her that the coppers had put Ron away for money laundering from one of the clubs. Ron was Jimmy's boss. He'd seen how much money there was; the club was just a cover. It was the fistfights and the gambling that made him rich. Jimmy was Ron's right-hand man. They were like brothers until he found out Ron had done the dirty on him with Pat. He only wanted what was rightfully his. He'd help Ron set the club up, did the tricks set the fights up, he was owed, and Susan was going to help him get his money. She snuggled into the pillow and felt herself drifting off to sleep.

There was a knock at the door. Linda was still reeling from the argument with Susan. She looked up from her book. "Who is it?" There was no answer. She opened the door. She saw her bike at the step. She caught a glance of Pat just getting into the car.

"Hey, Pat, wait…hey…open up."

Pat wound the window down and kept her sunglasses on. "Hi, Linda, I'm sorry I just wanted to drop the bike. I didn't expect you to come outside. I'm sorry, I have to be somewhere. I just wanted to drop it off for you, that's all. Now I must go."

Linda couldn't help but like Pat. She remembered how she'd given her a lift and had looked out for her. She didn't deserve to be treated the way she was by that Jimmy, and she didn't want Susan to run away with him. She hesitated, then spoke, "Pat, there's something you should know. It's about Jimmy and my sister. I need to tell you something; it's important."

Pat listened, stepped out of the car and took off her glasses. Linda took a gasp.

"My God! What's happened to your eyes?"

"It's nothing, darlin', just a punter. I had to throw out of one of my clubs, so what about your sister and Jimmy?" Pat swallowed hard. She didn't know what to expect although she did know that there was nothing she didn't know about Jimmy that would shock her. She prepared herself and waited.

"Susan and Jimmy are running away together, she told me. It's true, Pat, I told you 'cause you need to know. I don't want my sister to go, you understand that? I'm not telling you to hurt you…Say something please."

Pat was in shock, this wasn't true…no way! It's not part of the plan. He'd hurt her many times before, and she had him, but the last six months had been good. She winced as she put her sunglasses back on, reminding herself of his dark side and just how much he enjoyed inflicting pain.

"I don't believe you, Linda, you're jealous of Susan. You're making the whole thing up! Now I must go. I'm needed somewhere else." Pat slammed the door behind her. She drove away at speed she wasn't sure where she was going or what her next steps were, but deep in her heart, she knew Linda was most likely right. Ever since she'd had her miscarriage four months ago, Jimmy had changed. She was three months along at the time. A boy, a beautiful baby boy, ripped her heart out when she lost him. She blamed Jimmy for it. He'd heard about her affair with Ron and used her as a punching bag, said she deserved it. He could never totally be sure the kid would be his. He said they could start afresh, get the money from Ron he was owed and disappear. She believed him.

Pat's head was spinning. She needed to pull over. Her eyes filled with tears, recalling how very different it could have been for her if she hadn't had clapped eyes on Ron or Jimmy.

Chapter 9
In the Beginning

"Listen, Pat, I'm telling ya, girl, he's got his eye on you, an' that's all I'm saying. In fact, I bet you could take your pick of them both, a good-looker like you. Come on, Pat, let's go over to them and say hi…please?"

"Sal, I'm not interested 'av told ya, just leave it. If you wanna go over and introduce yourself, then go on. I'm not stopping you."

"Look, Pat, I'm not arguing with you or anything. I mean I was just fooling around and…oh, Pat, don't. Look now they're walking over to us! Shit."

Pat knew that coming to the 'Den' was a bad move tonight. She was tired and just wanted to let her hair down quietly at home, but Sal had other ideas. She'd heard that 'Den' was run by some nasty people, as her dad would say, and that they were wrong-uns to be involved with. The place itself inside the club was like a palace! Four floors combined with a giant dance floor on each and a 'men's only' club in the basement. The furnishings all velvet and gold and oozed expense. Girls all around, half-clad, hanging around the older men, all wanting a bit of glamour. Pat was different. She already had a club. She knew the tricks the girls would turn

31

and how these places really worked. Unlike little Sal who just wanted a night out in an upmarket club. She sighed, took a deep breath and turned to face the men who had just landed at her feet.

"Good evening, boys, my name's Sal, and this, here, is my good pal Pat."

Ron spoke first. His eyes were fixated on Pat. His stare was intense. His eyes were dark and deep. It was pat who pulled away.

"Evening, the pleasure is all mine' girls. Can I tempt you to a drink?" Ron clicked his fingers. Before they could reply, a young waiter came over with a tray full of Moet Champagne. Ron passed the girls two crystal flutes.

"Now we have the drinks; let me introduce myself; my name's Ron, and he's Jimmy." Jimmy didn't speak. He gave a half-smile and sipped his champagne.

"So, what brings you two lovely ladies to a club like this?"

"Well, Ron, it was my idea actually. I mean, every one raves about how great it is here. I needed to see for myself! I don't mind the price tag to get in, at least, I can say av been here. Oh, and Pat didn't want to come, did you, Pat? She's not one for these fancy clubs and…"

"OK, Sal, thanks. I can speak for myself." Pat felt nervous. Sal always ran her mouth and always seemed to make a show of her, even though it was never intentional! Sal was harmless, to say the least. God, she was her best friend, and after 15 years, you would think, she wouldn't get nervous when she's around, but Pat still did. They were like Jekyll and Hyde but loved each other deeply.

"Oh, is that so, Pat? You're not a fan of fancy clubs?"

Pat swallowed hard before she spoke. "Well, no, not really. I've been to a few, and I really don't enjoy them."

Jimmy turned to Pat and spoke, "What do you not enjoy, or rather what's not to enjoy?"

"Well, I actually have a club of my own. That was left to me by my father, and mine isn't fancy at all. It's real with hardworking people passing through them; not like this, this is so…so…blasé!"

"Well, well, well, I must say you have some attitude going on there, lady. I don't think I've ever recalled my club being called blasé; have you, Jimmy?"

Sal looked at Pat. They were definitely going to be thrown out! All the money she'd saved to pay to get in! Sal was seething. Jimmy looked at Pat and studied her before he spoke. "Hell no. Blasé? I'll show ya blasé; come here, listen, do you hear that it's the Lindi Hop. Come on, show me your moves." Before Pat could say 'no', she was pulled onto the giant revolving dance floor with Jimmy, and she was actually enjoying herself.

Pat jumped. *God, how long have I been asleep? It's dark*, she thought. Pat looked at her Cartier watch; another reminder of Jimmy. It's the real deal; well, at least, that's what he told her; probably something else to add to the list of lies he's been telling her. It was 8:25 p.m. pat looked in the car mirror and sighed. God, she looked rough! She needed to get her face on if she was gonna pay her old pal Ron a prison visit in a few days, but first, she needed a hand getting the Visiting Order.

Chapter 10

Pat

"Hey, Pat, well, I never! Long time, no see. I've not seen you for what four months? What brings you over here?" Sal was screeching with excitement. "Bloody hell, what's happened to your face? Has he beaten you up again? You look awful."

"Ah, Sal, can I come in, love, it's cold out here?"

"Sorry. Yes, of course. I'm just gobsmacked to see you. What's going on, Pat? Is everything OK? Where's Jimmy?"

Pat's face said it all. She was tired, and it was starting to take its toll on her good looks. Maybe that's why Jimmy was planning on leaving her because she looked haggard!

"Give me your coat lass; would you like a cuppa? Then we can have a long chat, what ya say?"

"Yeah, lovely, I'll have a coffee, Sal. God, I need the caffeine right now!"

Sal went to the kitchen to fix the drinks. Pat's eyes wandered around the room. She looked and looked until she'd found it. Aha, there it is. A group photo of the first night at the 'Den'. The four amigos together: RON and Jimmy, her and Sal. Pride of place on the dresser she should have known!

"Here ya go, Pat. Now come, sit down and talk to me. What's wrong?"

"Oh, Sal, I really don't know where to start." Pat sighed, then the tears came, and they wouldn't stop. "Basically, Jimmy's planning on leaving me. Yep, can you actually believe that he is leaving me?"

"No, I can't believe it. You've been through so much, and the miscarriage you told me about, has he no heart? I warned you about him, didn't I? You should have stayed with Ron. You could have had a different life, but no, you made your choice and broke Ron's heart. I don't think he'd ever forgive you for that. He's having an awful time in prison, ya know. I mean, obviously, he's living the life of Riley, what with him being a known local celeb an all and money isn't an option, but what I mean is he's not coping too well. It's not a nice place to go to, Pat. He writes to me every month, you know. The way it is with me and Ron, who'd have thought it…me and Ron friends till the end. I'm so sorry, sweetheart. I really am. What are you going to do?"

Pat's sobs had stifled. Her eyes were blackened from the Dior mascara that was supposed to be waterproof, hence the price tag. "I need you to do something for me, Sal. I need you to get me a visiting order to see Ron. Can you do that for me?"

"What do you want to see him for? He won't see ya, darlin', not after the miscarriage and that you know that he blames you. It's the best ya keep out the way?"

"Please, Sal, I'm begging ya. Just say it's for you! He needn't even know it's for me, please. I need to see him; the truth is I think I still love him. I need to see him, please."

"Let me sleep on it, love; it's getting late, and you're worn out. You can sleep in the spare room if ya like. It's all made up. Come on, let's go up to bed."

"Promise me you sleep on it, night, night."

Sal closed the door behind her, dived into her bed and snuggled the satin duvet up over her nose. Deep in thought, she imagined Ron's face when he sees Pat walking towards him. Who was she to stand in the way of true love! She was smiling as she drifted off to sleep. She'd already made her mind up.

Chapter 11
Jimmy

Jimmy stared at the phone in front of him. What was going on right now with Susan? The message he'd just listened to had left him furious. Wild thoughts were running in his mind. The truth is Jimmy hated being told what to do; he was used to calling the shots; he'd never listened to anybody in his life apart from Ron. Ron was his best mate, his life, his brother and partner in crime. Yeah, he didn't like some of the dealings Ron was mixed up in, but he went along with it all for the money. The money HIS money was yet to be seen. He wiped his forehead; he was sweating like a pig. He knew what he needed to do, he would do as Susan asked him, but he would also be paying Ron a visit…he wanted what he was owed…it's been a long time coming.

Chapter 12
Teddy

"Thanks, Gov, I'll be straight over to the station. I'll just grab my particulars."

"I'm off down the station love, don't wait up for me." Teddy grabbed his hat and coat and was in a hurry; the gov had something he wanted to see him about, and he was hoping it wasn't a reoccurrence of the previous night. He'd been watching Susan like a hawk over the last few days. He couldn't get it out of his head. There was no way Susan was involved with Jimmy. It was a mistake; it must have been. He'd tailed her every move, and no glimpse of Jimmy Jenkins. He was just about to close the front door when Nancy pulled the handle from the inside.

"Hey, if you think you're coming back here boozed-up like you did the other night, you be out on your ear! We got a reputation to keep up, and that 'Hoarse and Hound' ought to be shut down. I'm warning you, Teddy, any more nonsense like that, and you're out. I won't have it. I know what goes on down there. Do you hear me?"

Teddy looked at Nancy through his glasses and smiled. He was so lucky to have Nancy. She could have had anybody she wanted. She was beautiful even when she was mad at him.

Her eyes were piercing green, and with her long red hair, she was a beauty. He stepped through the door and pulled her close. "I love you, Nancy. See you when I get back, love."

"Right, Gov, what's up? Is it this Jimmy Jenkins' business again? 'cause I can tell you now I've tailed her myself and…"

"All right, now, Cartwright, take a seat and settle in, man. let me speak," The Gov was wary of Teddy, especially after what he'd heard about the night at the 'Hoarse and Hound'. He would have to be careful and very tactful.

"Teddy, I'm going to ask you a question, and I want you to be honest with me, please…Are you having relations with Pat Noon?"

"Certainly not, sir. I can reassure you now. I don't know how you can insinuate such a thing. I love my Nancy. We've been together for over twenty years. Where's this came from, I don't understand?"

"Bluewater saw you two together, said you looked very cosy. In actual fact, you were that cosy you stayed the night with her in the hotel room above."

Teddy was white as a sheet. He couldn't remember, and that was the truth of it. He'd played the night over and over again in his head, and he got the same answer: he really couldn't remember. "That's rubbish! What would I want with Pat Noon?"

"Teddy, you have to see it from our view. Your daughter has been linked to Jimmy Jenkins, Ron's right-hand man, and now you are canoodling with Noon, his girlfriend; how do you think this looks, man?" The gov banged his fists on the desk; he was red in the face. His long-standing reputation was on the line if any of this was found to be true. He studied Teddy's face; he could tell a liar after all he had a lot of years' experience; however, Teddy's face was hard to read. He was expressionless and deep in thought. It took a while before he replied:

"Gov, I'm gonna tell you the truth. I can't remember! I know what you're gonna think, but I was bladdered, you know. I'd had a bad day, and I wanted to let off some steam. I had a couple and she turned up. We chatted; she spoke about Jimmy, and I thought she might spill some beans here about the missing money. I was out of my mind, Gov, I'm sorry. I can't remember anything else."

"I suggest you start remembering and fast. If you have leaked any of the investigations to her, Jimmy and Ron could get off Scot-free, and you can kiss your promotion goodbye. On the other hand, if you can find out where the money is and start collecting enough evidence to keep Ron inside for good and put Jimmy away, then and only then you may still be in with a chance. Right now, I don't think you are aware of your actions and how you have jeopardised the whole investigation. I'm keeping a very close eye on you, Teddy, and if you so much as put one foot out of line or meet up with Noon on any occasion, you will be in for the chop. Do I make myself clear?"

"Loud and clear, I'll see myself out then."

"Get out."

It wasn't until the door closed that the gov lit a Marlboro and poured himself a straight Jamison whiskey. He sighed. Something wasn't right. He just couldn't put his finger on it.

Just then a call came in…

"Gov, it's Bluewater. I've just finished tailing Pat Noon. You never guess where she is…HMO DURHAM PRISON."

"I'm guessing she's paying Ron a visit, don't you, Bluewater?"

Chapter 13
Ron

Ron couldn't believe it; after four months of begging, Sal to come to see him; today would be the day. He stared, looking at the unopened letters he had piled up from Jimmy. He never opened them because he knew what they would say...You see, they were like brothers, him and Jimmy, until Pat got in the way. He'd been stupid to betray Jimmy with Pat, but the truth was he loved her and still did. That's why he'd taken all the blame when the coppers raided the club and found the money; he did it for Jimmy. He owed him in a big way, and no amount of money was gonna put that right. He smiled. At least, the money was somewhere safe, ready for when he got out. It was safe all right.

"Hey, Ron! Get your glad rags on, mate; there's a woman here to see ya; a fancy one n all."

Prison officer Davies liked Ron. He kept the wing in check, and he was treated like a king in there.

"I'm ready, Davies; take me down."

Ron had forgotten what a woman looked like in the flesh! He had pictures of Sal and a one of his mum before she died, but the one photo he always kept under his pillow was Pat. He sat down ready for his visit, and when he saw the angel that was walking towards him, he nearly fell back off his chair.

"My, oh my…my darlin' Pat. What are you doing here? It's no place for a lady."

"Oh, Ron, I had to see you. Please, forgive Sal; she sorted the VO for me. I made her do it. I knew you wouldn't have seen me. I needed to see you. There's so much happened since you've been inside." Pat was teary, her eye still largely swollen from Jimmy. Ron knew he had given her a beating again. She didn't have to tell him. He knew it was Jimmy's style.

"Like Jimmy still beating the crap out of ya? I can't understand why you've come here, Pat. It's not a nice place to be in."

"Ron, I need you to know, Archie was your son. It's been haunting me since I lost him. Jimmy would kill me if he knew I told you. I don't expect you to believe me, but I wanted you to know. There's other stuff, Ron, big stuff that you don't know about him. Like how he set you up so you would get put in here, so he could run with the money. But it backfired Ron, didn't it? Because there was no money at the club, he knew the combinations, though he had seen the money over two million quid, Ron, in the safe the night you got arrested. Less than two hours later, the safe was empty, and no one else apart from you and Jimmy knew them combinations. Am I right, Ron?"

Ron's eyes fixated on Pat's red thin lips; her mouth was moving but he blocked out her voice; he had to think of something fast to shut her up.

"Look, Pat, we have a history together. I loved you. The truth is I still do, but do you really think I'm stupid?"

There was a long silence, then Pat spoke, "Ron, what did you mean when you said do you think I'm stupid?"

"Jimmy set me up! I'm one step ahead of him all the way, Pat. Do you not think I don't sit here day after day thinking how I'm gonna get out of here? And what I'm gonna do to him? He was my best mate, Pat, and we betrayed him. You sit here now and tell me Archie was my son? Do you really know that, Pat? Do you? What do you want from me eh? money?"

Ron's voice was becoming louder and louder. He was mad, really mad. Pat could see the anger in his eyes. It was her fault, she knew it, but she had to see Ron and tell him about Archie. It was only right if he knew. She pulled on her coat. "Right, I've come and said what I needed to say; please don't hate me, Ron. I've never stopped loving you, and it kills me to think of you in here. We could have had a good life; you and me. I'm sorry, sorry for everything." Pat turned away. She didn't want Ron to see her tears, after all, she was hard as nails; she was Pat…That's what she kept telling herself. As she turned to walk away, Ron spoke:

"Pat, please sit back down, love. We can talk through our differences, girl. I apologise I shouldn't have raised my voice to you. It's this place, messes with your head, you know what I mean?"

"Look at me, I'm a mess. You know how I liked my suits and tie. Well, these prison scrubs are well out my league." They laughed and Pat sat back down. She looked around in dismay at the other inmates, wondering what they'd done to land themselves a bit of time in the nick. She decided there and then she was going to do what it takes to get Ron out. She owed him that at least. She looked at Ron. He was so handsome even in here, those eyes, his jet-black hair gelled back as usual into his ducktail at the back of his head. He was clean-shaven as always. He looked exactly the same as always, apart from the clothing attire, of course. She took a deep breath and said,

"Ron, I'm gonna get you out of here, love."

Chapter 14
Teddy

Teddy settled himself into bed. Nancy hadn't waited up for him. She was already asleep by the time he'd got back from the station. He had replayed every bit of his conversation with Pat Noon that he could remember, and still nothing. He needed to remember and fast. The guv was going spare at him, had really made him think he could actually lose his job if he'd jeopardised the whole investigation. He looked at the clock. It was 2:40 a.m. He could feel himself drifting to sleep; all the while Pat Noon was on his mind. He could hear her voice loud and clear…

"So, what's a nice man like you doing in here?"

"Drowning my sorrows, so to speak, what brings you here? It certainly can't be the clientele, love, you look to descent to be from around here."

"Well, thank you. I do take pride in my appearance. Listen, I'm celebrating; would you like a whiskey?"

"I shouldn't, I should get back as you can see I'm pretty rat-arsed and my wife will have my guts when I get home."

"That's a shame. I thought me and you could drown our sorrows together; it's not often you meet someone of intelligence around here to talk to, if ya know what I mean?"

"Ah, OK then, you've twisted my arm. I'll have one, and that's it mind; let's call it one for the road. Make it a double, lass." Pat's plan was working. She got Timmy to slip some of that white powder he sold into Teddy's drink, that got him talking for sure. She walked over to the bar and shouted:

"Timmy, hey Timmy, give it a double jack Daniels in here and a bit of the white fairy in too, if ya don't mind."

Timmy was hesitant of Pat, he thought before he spoke, "Who's it for, Pat? Is it for you?"

"It's for him, you moron," she pointed to Teddy who was slumped over the table.

"I don't think it's a good idea, Pat. Look at him; he's out for the counts. He's had a ton; leave him. Get yourself back to Jimmy; he'll be wondering where you are, man."

Pat was raging Jimmy didn't want her, and now she decided nor did she want him.

"Put it in the drink, Timmy; I'm asking you nicely. I won't ask nicely again. If ya don't, I'll tell Jimmy ya trying it on with me again, and he won't be too pleased about that, will he?"

Timmy reluctantly handed over the drinks and watched from the corner of the bar while Pat canoodled with the DCI. Oh, what a story he would have to tell Jimmy, and he wouldn't be too pleased about that Pat Noon!

Pat walked over to the table and plonked the drinks down, remembering which one was supposed to be for Teddy.

"So, what ya celebrating then? Can I ask?"

"Well, I'm celebrating the upcoming release of my dear friend, he's been away inside at Durham for around four months now. I miss him like crazy."

"Well, that's got to be worth celebrating; what's he been inside for, love?"

"Ah, this and that. you see…sorry, I didn't catch your name…"

"Teddy, Teddy Cartwright. Pleased to meet you."

"Come on have a toast with me, would you? Let's raise a glass to all of us who've been betrayed once in a while."

"I'll drink to that."

Teddy knocked back the drink…the rest was a blur…he's in a room not sure where; he could hear his name being called…Teddy was in the bathroom, his clothing was undone, and he was lying in the bath. Where was he? He couldn't remember getting here? What happened?

Teddy jumped; his alarm clock had gone off. He looked at the clock. "Christ, 5:55 a.m." He'd had a few hours' sleep but was none the wiser as to what had happened that night in the 'Hoarse and Hound'. What information if any he had given to Pat. He took a deep breath; he was wide awake. He got up and walked into his office. He took the key from under the loose floorboard and turned the lock to his drawer.

It was still there; it was right where he'd left it. As long as Ron was banged up and he was still on the case, he had nothing to worry about.

Teddy smiled…It was all his.

Part 2

December 1951

Ron looked out onto the street below the club. The Christmas decorations were already starting to go up! His favourite time of the year. The tree was up in the square and the lights twinkled blue and white. There were kids everywhere, and a group of carol singers gathered around the tree, ready to belt out a song. He smiled. He loved Christmas. It brought back fond memories. Even when he had nothing as a kid, his parents had always done their best and embraced Ron with love and the true meaning of Christmas. It was only when he heard the knock on his office door that he realised he was crying. He quickly wiped his eyes and lit a cigar. He stood up, then looked in the mirror. "Clear yourself up, Ron; you daft sod, you got work to do." Just then Jimmy walked in…

"Ron, you OK, mate?"

"What you doing back, Jimmy? I told ya to go and collect. I'm sick of doing all the running about. I tell ya to do one thing, Jimmy, and you can't even do that! What's the matter with you these days? Fucking posing around with the women that's what. You got Pat. What the fuck you want more for?"

Ron's eyes were bulging. He was wild-eyed, and Jimmy didn't know where this outburst had come from. At first, he thought he might have run out of sniff, then he remembered

Ron hadn't touched a thing since they bought the club two years back. He had to tread carefully; after all, Ron was the one with brains.

"What's up, mate? Is it the money? Has it not come through yet?"

"Shut up, Jimmy; this is your fucking fault. The money should have been here at 11. It's now bloody 12. Look at me, Jimmy, for the first time in my life, I'm sweating. Look at my hands. I can feel it, Jimmy, summit's up; summit's not right. If this deal doesn't go down, we're goosed the lot of us. Do you understand that, Jimmy? It was supposed to be a make or break deal; our whole future mapped out before us, our dream. We could never make that money going clean in a million years. You said you could trust this contact, so where the fuck is he? I gave you one job, Jimmy, one; like I said, don't make me live to regret it."

Jimmy was scared; the sight of Ron losing control was not a pretty sight. His mind was working overtime. That deal was watertight he'd made sure of it. He took a long look at Ron who was now pacing the floor and fiddling with his hair.

"Give over, Ron; they'll be here soon; they're just late; that's all…"

Jimmy's voice trailed off. Ron wasn't listening. He was deep in thought. Jimmy thought back to a call he had overheard the day before…was there more to this deal than his Ron was letting on? He played it over in his mind…

Tom

"Tom, I ain't asking ya; I'm telling ya. I want security on; what's in it for me and Jimmy? I need facts and info; meet me at Hawkins bar in town 9:30, Saturday, and we can go from there. I want to know who I'm working with, and if they have my readies. Listen, Tom, Jimmy doesn't know I'm doing this. It's just I like to be in control. It's a big deal, Tom, you know what I mean, don't ya?"

"OK, Ron, mate, I'll do my best honest, ya know my hands are tied on how much I can tell ya, but I'll see ya Saturday; you can count on me."

Tom placed the phone down. It was a cold night. He lit a cigarette (no 9) and opened the telephone box door. His mind was racing full of the conversation he'd just had. He'd forgotten to pick up his note confirming the details for Saturday. He turned back towards the phone box; his pace quickened. It was a cold night; he could see his breath. He saw the headlights approaching. He turned to see who it was…it was too late.

The car ran over his lifeless body four times forwards and backwards just to make sure he was dead.

One down, two to go.

Jimmy

Jimmy listened quietly. He'd just overheard Ron on the blower, and he wanted to know more. He knocked on Ron's door and waited…

"Come."

"Hey, I've been thinking, Ron, what do ya say me and you go into town Saturday? Like the good old days eh? We haven't got bladdered for a while, and there's plenty of skirt to keep us busy. what do ya say?"

Ron kept his eyes fixated on the newspaper in front of him, so he didn't have to look Jimmy in the eye. He hated keeping secrets from Jimmy. He was a brother to him; however, Jimmy had a big mouth, so some things he didn't know about were for his own good.

"Ah, I don't think so, Jimmy, son; I've got a bit of business to sort, but I tell ya what I'll see how I get on and meet you later. why don't ya ask Wayne to go with ya? He loves the plonk, and he's a great laugh."

Jimmy was hurt. He looked at Ron and spoke, "What business ya got on that I don't know about?"

"Nothing for you to worry about, Jimmy; all in good time; now go on and collect from the 'Hoarse and Hound'. They owe us a ton, and if they don't pay up, this time set Wayne onto Tim. It's about time they knew who owned that joint. It's been a long time coming we've given them time, but Jimmy, mate, time's running out for them. Put the frighteners on them, Jimmy. We need that money…"

"I'm on it, Ron. I best be off then. I'll see ya."

Jimmy closed the door behind him; his mind was racing. What was going on here? The conversation he'd overheard confirmed a meeting in town Saturday, and Ron was saying he was busy? Ron's not telling the truth, why? They were a team; why the sudden secrecy? They were brothers, and brothers don't keep secrets. He shook the thoughts from his mind…if only he knew…if only…TEDDY…

"Teddy love, breakfast is ready. Come on, it's getting cold." Teddy was looking forward to his breakfast he'd been called out late last night, and he'd only had a few hours kip, but he was starving. His stomach rumbled and his Nancy did make the best eggs ever. He dressed and dragged himself down the stairs. He sat in his usual spot at the table with the best view of the garden; even though it was December, he could still see his blue tit in the garden. He laughed and shook his head seeing bloody birds. He got that from his father. He was a keen bird watcher, it wasn't until Teddy was in his late twenties that he realised it wasn't that kind of bird watching his father liked. He looked around for the usual morning paper...

"Nancy love, where's the morning paper?"

"It's on the bench near the sink. I'll get it, Teddy."

"There you go, would you look at that. Teddy? What a waste of a life! It's frontpage look."

Teddy studied the front page. The headline was HIT AND RUN. He wolfed his breakfast down. He realised something was missing. "Where's the tea, Nancy? Where are the girls, are they coming down for breakfast? You're too soft on them, Nancy. I've told you before. They should be down here first shout."

"Like you are, Teddy? You should watch what you say." Teddy wasn't listening to Nancy. He shuddered as he recalled the sight of Tom, a local no-mark, who had met his end last night. In his twenty years of policing, he'd never seen a sight like he had last night from a hit and run. Whoever had done it, had done a bloody good job. Poor lad was unrecognisable; every bone in his body crushed along with his skull. Such a brutal attack on such a young lad. The question was why was he dead. He thought back to the scene last night. He was first on the scene with DCI Bluewater.

"Poor sod. Looks like whoever did this has done it good and proper, sir."

"Do we have any witnesses yet, Bluewater? Who found him?"

"Here's over there, Cartwright, said he was walking to the phonebook to make a call, his mother's not to well, so he was gonna call the doctor. It was just after midnight. He approached the phone box and saw him lying in the road. He's well shook up. He called us straightaway and called the doctor for his mother."

"What's his name?"

"Erm…that would be Charlie…Charlie Small. He lives in the flats over on thorny close, sir; about five minutes from here."

"Right! Get him down the nick and find out all you can. Bluewater, no stone unturned, you got me? The coroner should be here in a few minutes. I'll get one of the boys to stay here with the coroner; keep me informed all the way, and I'll see you in the morning."

DCI Bluewater didn't like taking orders from Teddy; however, he was biding his time until the time was right to spill the beans on a little secret he knew about Teddy. He would play that hand when he needed to, and keep it close to his chest.

****

Teddy realised he'd finished his breakfast. He looked around. Linda was sitting, scoffing a cold breakfast and Susan was on the telephone. Nancy noticed Teddy was quiet. She looked at him. He wasn't himself this morning. He was too quiet. She spoke softly, "Teddy, are you all right? You're not yourself this morning. Is it that job you got called out to last night? What is it? You can tell me, love."

"You're right. I am thinking about that poor lad. It's on the front cover the HIT AND RUN article. It's the call out I did last night. I don't think he was even a year older than the twins. What a waste of a life, Nancy."

"What was his name, Teddy? Do you know anything about him?"

"All we know is his name was Tom. There was a driver's licence in his jeans pocket. Looks like he was a local lad from Hall Lane Estate."

Linda dropped her knife and fork and screamed. She ran from the table upstairs to her room and slammed the door behind her. She felt as if her heart was being ripped out of her chest. She sobbed not her Tom. It can't be…her one and only love…

Teddy wasn't daft. He knew the name had hit a nerve with Linda. He flashed a look at Nancy and waited for her to run upstairs after her, as if on cue, she waited for Teddy to finish his cuppa before she spoke.

"You don't think our Linda was, you know, having relations with this Tom, do you? The scream and the way she ran upstairs, it looked like she was in shock, Teddy, and don't tell me you can't hear her crying either."

Nancy's mouth was moving, but Teddy couldn't hear her voice. He was recalling the moment he stood over that poor lad last night. He shuddered. How was he going to tell his parents that their kid was dead. Why was he bothered? It was like water off a duck's back he'd done a thousand times before, so what was different now? He would have to look them in the eye and tell them their beloved son was dead and never coming back. How would he feel if that was Susan or Linda? He was getting old and going soft. He only snapped out of his daydream when Nancy slammed his plate onto the sink. "Are you listening? Your daughter is upstairs breaking her heart up there. Are you going up to see her or not?"

Teddy rose from his seat. He looked over at Nancy. He was so lucky to have her.

"On my way, darling." As he climbed the stairs, he thought about what Linda might tell him. He didn't want to know; however, he needed to know. He prepared himself. As he got to the top stair, he could hear the sobbing coming from Linda's room. It was louder now. He knocked and waited. It wasn't until the third knock that she answered the door and lay back on the bed. It was Teddy who spoke first.

"Linda love, can I ask you, are you upset about Tom? Please tell me you didn't know him, Linda? Come on, tell me. I don't like to see you upset. You can tell me anything, darlin'. You know that, remember I'm your dad before a police officer."

Linda's cries came to a stop. She turned her head towards Teddy and wiped her eyes with her sleeve. She took a deep breath and sat up straight.

"Dad, Tom was my boyfriend. I know you hate us mixing with no-marks, but Dad, I swear he wasn't bad. He wouldn't hurt a fly. Why would someone do this, Daddy, why? I didn't tell you or Mum about us. I'm sorry, Dad, I wish I had. He's dead, and I loved him, and I don't know what I'm going to do." Linda started to cry once more. This time, she buried her head into her pillow. She didn't want her dad to see her cry. Teddy turned her to face him. Her eyes were wide open, red and swollen from cries, her nose running. She looked so lost and defeated. Teddy hugged her.

"You'll be all right, girl. I promise you, I'll find out who did this; you mark my words, I will find out."

****

"Boss, it's me. Listen, we done the job good and proper. He's finished. The papers will get the story Hit and Run, and yeah, we made sure we covered our tracks. We got the meeting details, so looks like we be paying our old friend Ron a surprise visit."

****

Ron

Ron caught a glimpse of himself in the car mirror. *Ouch what a handsome bloke I am*, he thought. Suited and booted in his best attire, he was ready for business. He checked his teeth (that had cost him more than a ton) whiter than white. He smiled. He loved himself. He took care of himself; nothing wrong with that; he just didn't have a woman. There was only one woman for Ron, and she'd made her choice loud and clear, probably for the best seen as though Jimmy was like a brother. It was over, Pat made sure of that. Time to move on, Ron old son.

He checked his watch. It was 12:10. He had plenty of time to park the car and head straight for the meeting. He was close to closing this deal, and he was hoping Tom had the answers he was looking for. He turned into central station and headed for the car park. He wasn't sure, but he thought he saw someone he knew from back when he was just starting out, he drove slowly through the car park to have a look. Yeah, he was right. It was his old mate Trev. They did time together a few years back. What the fuck was he doing around here? More to the point, who was he working for now? Ron didn't bother stopping; he kept his distance and parked on the top floor; this would give him a view of the pub so he could plan an escape route if needed. He always did this. It was always being one step ahead, and in Ron's game, that could be a matter of life or death. He checked his inside pocket. His COLT pistol was right there and ready for business (should he need it, of course). He took his comb from his pocket and combed his hair. He always did it before a meeting; it was a habit. He locked the car up and walked out onto the street. It was busy with Christmas stalls and kids visiting Santa. He breathed the air in and smiled…that was the smell of Christmas. He chuckled. Before he knew it, he was at the door of the pub. He hesitated and walked in. He looked at the huge clock on the wall; 12:25. He was early! He approached the bar and quickly ordered a scotch. Well, he did have five minutes to kill. He downed it in one and asked for another. Just as he was swigging the last dregs, he heard a familiar voice…

"Well, I'll be, if it isn't my old mate Ron, how ya doing, mate?"

****

Trevor

Ron was confused. What the hell was he doing here? Twice in one day, first the car park, now here. Trev of all people and of all the days, this could mess up his plans. Trevor approached Ron, and before he knew it, Trev had his hand on his shoulder. "Long time no see, mate; must be what six years since I've seen ya; here let me buy ya a drink; what you doing in town?" Ron hesitated. He had to think of something fast.

"Hey, Trev, good to see ya. I'm meeting a bird, ain't I? Look I would love to stay and chat, mate, but I best be off."

"Come on, Ron, you can do better than that; how about me and you grab a scotch and sit around the back somewhere? We can't be disturbed. There's a back door here. We can have a game of poker or summit just like old times?"

"Like I said, Trev, I best be off…" Ron caught a glimpse of what looked like an outline of a gun in Trev's pocket. He was now thinking of that escape route. "Look, Trev, what is it? What do ya want?"

"I've got a message for ya int I from Tom…"

Ron's eyes were wide open when he heard Tom's name. He was like a wild man. He had to think fast. He did a quick check of the exit in front of him and decided that he'd go for the one out the back. He wasn't going out with a bullet in his back; no way. He paused and composed himself. He ran his fingers through his hair. *Shit*, he thought…*I've been set up*. Trevor was just about to open his mouth again and Ron spoke quickly, "Look, Trev, really nice meeting ya, mate, honestly it is, if you've got a message from Tom for me, then where is it? I'm running late to meet my bird, so if ya wouldn't mind…" Ron stood up from the stool. He had no intention of walking out the front door. He knew what was coming to him; he wasn't daft.

"Ron, Tom wants ya to know you've been set up, mate, so if ya wouldn't mind coming with me, we got to be somewhere." Ron pulled his pistol out and pointed it at Trev. He was fast; he had it whipped out within seconds. He could shoot him there and then, but that wasn't Ron's style. He pointed the trigger at Trev's head; he could see the fear on the barmaid's face and the punters sitting beside them; he needed them out; he had to think fast…he let the gun off and shouted:

"Everyone fuckin out now!" Within seconds, the bar was cleared, he sat Trev down in the corner of the bar and took his gun from his pocket.

"Right, Trev, now there's just me and you and the jukebox. We're gonna play a little trip down memory lane, so I'll start first and you answer, got it?"

Trevor was frightened for all he was meant to do was deliver a message; nothing else, who better to deliver it than him? They did time together. He didn't want to hurt Ron. "Question one, Trev, Where's Tom?"

"He's dead, Ron, hit and Run. It'll be in the papers tomorrow. The boss said you need to come with me if you want your money."

"Dead? What do ya mean fuckin dead, why? What did he do to anyone? He's just a kid!"

"He saw summit he shouldn't have, so the boss wanted rid, ya know how it is."

Ron wasn't soft, but he felt his eyes well up. He was just a kid; just a kid; his whole life was in front of him; the bastards. His eyes bulged.

"Who's the boss, Trev? WHO IS HE? TELL ME OR I SWEAR I WILL BLOW YOUR BRAINS OUT."

Trevor was terrified. He didn't sign up for this. He was going to have to tell him. He opened his mouth. Just as he was about to speak, a bullet hit him straight in the forehead. He was dead within seconds. Ron looked around him. *Shit! where the fuck did that come from?* He thought. He was being watched. He quickly ran towards the back exit. He ran all the way back to the car. He could hear the police sirens in the air. He jumped in the driver's seat and fired her up, speed all the way back to the club. What he didn't realise that on the way, he'd dropped his beloved Colt Revolver…

****

Teddy

Teddy made the usual 25-minute journey into the station as he did every morning, however, this morning seemed like it took forever. His daughter Linda was laying heavy on his mind, and the promise he'd kept her wasn't going to be an easy one to keep. He needed to keep this to himself; the guv or Bluewater wasn't to know. He knew he'd be risking his job, but his promise had to be kept whichever way he looked at it. Just as Teddy was turning into the station, DCI Bluewater was standing with the guv and the press at the station doors. Teddy muttered under his breath, this was one of the worst parts of the job, laying down the gory details to the scavengers as he liked to call them. He parked up in his usual spot and made his way over to the entrance…

"Morning, Guv."

"Ah! DCI Cartwright, can I have a word? Shall we? Inside, of course; Bluewater, can you take over from here please, just a few details left to confirm, and then get them out of here."

"Yes, Guv, no problem." Bluewater basked in confirming all the gory details on the Hit and Run. He enjoyed the feeling of power. Soon he would have that power...

Teddy wasn't very alert this morning, Linda had cried herself to sleep, and he'd heard every cry; he jolted when the guv opened the station door.

"Yes, sir; is there a problem, sir?"

The Guv led the way down the dingy corridor into his office and closed the door behind Teddy.

"Teddy, can I ask you to take a seat? I've an update on the hit and run last night, and I wanted you to be the first to know my findings. If you are to take over from me when I retire in a few years, Teddy, I need you to be on my side. Do you understand?" Teddy was wide-eyed; what was the Guv talking about, and why has Bluewater not been told this?

"Yes, Guv, you have my word; please go on..."

"Well, Teddy, we've had a report on the tyre tracks last night; as you know, it was cold night and the rain did wash most of the marks away, however, the car upped onto part of the grass verge just in front of the telephone box and we have a match on the tyre print. With that, and our eyewitness, we've narrowed the make and model down to a Jaguar MKX-One registration number BYD 185B. I have had a report, Teddy, that the car in question is registered to DCI Bluewater. Now we need to keep this between us for now, Teddy.

"I'm sure you will agree until I can think what the next step with Bluewater will be. Can I count on you, Teddy? I will need your cooperation and total secrecy on this."

Teddy couldn't believe his ears. He wanted to shout out: no, that can't be right; it's a mistake. He was now having a flash back to the night Bluewater was first on the scene, already there and the lad the eyewitness, he was already there and crying and not making sense. Suddenly, he was painting a totally different picture to the scene of the crime with most probably the eyewitness as the killer and Bluewater involved. His mind was racing; he stood up and spoke,

"Gov, you seriously don't think he's involved, do you? It must be a mistake, I mean, I know I always said he was a bit dodgy, but I didn't mean it."

"Teddy, we have been tailing Bluewater over a period of months, and there is evidence of corruption; now off you go, and not a word to anyone! Shut the door on the way out."

"Gov, you said an eyewitness; was it the young lad at the scene?"

"To the contrary, we have had a young lady anonymous come forward telephoned the station this morning, she said she saw who was driving the car at the time."

"We surely can't proceed on a tip off, Guv?"

"I will be the judge of that; now off you go and make sure you get plenty of coffee down your neck or a stiff brandy; you look like dead!"

With Teddy gone, the Guv was pondering over what he had found out this morning; it didn't make sense? Why would the car be registered to Bluewater; surely, he would know he would be found out; only a matter of time. He poured himself a coffee and glanced at the newspaper on his desk HIT AND

RUN. Well, it looked like he could be making an arrest soon, and it was going to be a very enjoyable one. Obviously, Bluewater would get what's coming to him if he can't prove otherwise, but he's been after this no-mark for the last two years, and he couldn't be happier to make the arrest.

****

He couldn't wait to make the call; he needed the money. He wasn't sorry for any of it. He smoked his cigar and dialled the number.

"Boss, it's me; it's done. She's made the call; it is only a matter of time. I'll keep you posted of our next steps."

Ron

Ron was laying low; it had been a few days since the shootout, with no sign of any money coming, he realised he'd been had! The deal he thought Tom had set up was fake; he was out of pocket by 25k; how was he going to tell Jimmy? He couldn't get his head around it all; nothing was making sense. Jimmy had done a moon light flit, and Pat had no idea where he could be. He kept thinking about that day, the meeting, tom, his old mate, his beloved revolver that was now missing. He was frightened when he'd read the article in the local standard on the HIT AND RUN, and it was there in black and white. Tom was dead, whoever was tailing Tom knew the meeting details; they had to. That Bullet that day was meant for Ron, he was certain; the question was who fired it. He stirred from his daydream to hear a commotion downstairs in the club. He heard footsteps coming upstairs getting closer to him, as quick as he moved to lock the door, it was burst open.

"Ron Curry, I'm arresting you in connection with the death of Tom Green-wall; you do not have to say anything that may…" Ron wasn't listening. The arrest was a blur; it only hit him when the handcuffs were on and he was frogmarched out in the club and out into the waiting police escort. He looked at the arresting officer; he thought he knew him; his mind was ticking over big time now. He was being framed; the question was: by who?

Jimmy and Pat

"Look, Jimmy, I did my bit, and I'm not testifying on Ron; you can beat me, do whatever you like to me; you will anyway!!!" Pat was thinking of what she had done; why the hell did she agree to go along with it in the first place? Jimmy, that's why, she was head over heels in love with him and just couldn't live without him. Even after a short fling with Ron, he took her back. She hated him for making her lose her baby, but he was like a drug. The temper, the violence, the clubs, it's all she knew. She lied for Jimmy so many times. She knew never to ask questions, but after she'd rung the station like Jimmy told her to and say Ron was driving the HIT AND RUN vehicle, she knew she had made a big mistake. Now she would pay the price if Jimmy didn't like what she was saying she'd know about it soon enough. She waited for Jimmy to emerge from the shower; he was ashen-faced and looked quite feeble in an unusual way.

"Ya right, Darlin'? It was wrong of me to ask ya to do that, but ya know Ron's been cutting me out of deals for the last few months; he's crossed the line, Pat. I found another seven invoices in his drawer; I'm owed close to five hundred smackers. With Ron out the way, I can take his cut swell, that's nearing a million quid. Imagine the life we can have, the new start? Get away from here, leave this shit hole behind. Ya know the reason I asked ya, you're coming with me. I never thought in a million years about doing the dirty on my Ron, but he's done it to me, Pat. I got the proof." Pat believed every word he said, and why wouldn't she? She trusted him. Her heart strings played on the fact that Ron was a mate and ex-lover but Jimmy was her life. He was all she needed, and they would see this plan out, she had to; she decided she would go to the station and testify…she had to…

Teddy

Teddy had the job waiting for the anonymous caller to come in for an interview. He looked at the clock on the hideous yellow wall; it was 13:20; she was late by five minutes. He had a lot of questions to ask, but he must tread carefully. He hadn't forgotten that promise he made to Linda either; he vowed to catch the killer who took away the love of her life. That promise was at the front of his mind, and he was hoping this lady had the answers to a lot of question. Just then there was a knock at the door. "DCI Cartwright, I have a Miss Gloria Eustin for you, sir; she's a few minutes late. Shall I bring her straight through?"

"Yes, send her in Mathews and bring us some coffee, will you?"

"Right away, sir."

"Good afternoon, Miss Eustin. My name is Detective Inspector Cartwright. Please take a seat; make yourself comfortable, and we can make a start."

Teddy offered her the coffee that was just brought in from Mathews and made himself comfortable. He stared at her; he was sure he'd seen her somewhere before but just didn't know where; anyway, he had a job to do, so time to get down to business. "Miss Eustin, can I start by asking you where you were on the night of the Hit and Run?"

"Why, yes, I was walking from the corner shop just on edge of the road where I'd been to buy some cigarettes."

"Would the shop keeper remember you being there?"

"I would think so; in fact, I do remember him saying I was the only person that had been in the shop in the last half hour. It was that dead 'cause of the weather and that."

"Can you tell me what time this was?"

"I can't say for certain, but it was probably around eightish."

"OK, so now we have your movements. Was there anybody else who saw you either leaving the shop or waking towards the scene of the crime?"

Pat thought long and hard, she knew whatever answers from now would be made up; however, she didn't really know if anyone had seen her in the shop at all.

"No, not that I'm aware of."

"Can I ask where you went after you left the shop?"

"Yeah, I headed towards Burnley Avenue; it was really cold, and I remember I was walking very fast; it was a mile down the road. I heard a screech just near the telephone box. I glanced across. I could see a lad lying in the road, and a car driving back and forth over him."

"Could you see the driver?"

"Yes?"

"Well, who was it you saw?"

"It was Ron, Ron Curry…"

It was done now; Pat was disgusted she'd told bare face lies to the police. Jimmy had filled her in on what to say; he even helped her with the disguise; she wondered how he knew all the details if he wasn't there like he said? She signed her witness statement in her false name and hoped it would get Ron put away. She walked out of the station and was amazed to find Jimmy waiting for her. She smiled. He jumped out the car and gave her a big wink.

"How did ya do, girl? Did they believe ya?"

"I think so; he asked me all about the shop keeper and if he would remember me being in the shop that night, and I think he believed me!"

"Jump in, ma darlin'; don't worry about the shopkeeper. I'll bang him a ton and he'll say anything I want him to, ya did well, ma darlin'; all we need to do now is sit back and wait…"

Teddy was finishing up after the interview; he'd seen the Guv and filled him in, and it looked pretty certain Ron would be charged with the murder. He wasn't sure as yet what part in all this Bluewater was playing, but he would soon enough find out. Just as he was about to head off, Bluewater appeared.

"Teddy, alright? Where ya off? Are ya done now?" Bluewater was making small talk with Teddy; he could sense something was up.

"Yes, I'm…er…off to take the twins and the Mrs out for tea; I'm in a rush, so I'll see ya tomorrow." Teddy walked straight past Bluewater and couldn't wait to get home. He had a bad feeling about him; he'd had it since the day he joined the station'; he was what you would call an odd ball. Looking back, he always seemed to have plenty of grassers and snouts on the streets. He seemed to know a lot for being an odd ball. He would speak to the Guv tomorrow, he decided, and see what course of action needed to be taken with regards to Bluewater. He needed to get home and relax, most importantly, see his girls.

Ron

Ron was waiting to be told his fate; he was shaking. He knew what happened to people like him inside. It didn't seem to matter how many times he said he didn't kill Tom and he wasn't there. The police had their statement from an eyewitness that saw Ron mow Tom down. Jimmy had been nowhere in sight; he'd tried to make his call home to Jimmy at the club, but there wasn't an answer; he was Ron's alibi.

He was frightened like never before. *Who could do this to me?* he thought, *and why?* He hung his head and waited, and waited, and waited. He even thought they were going to come out and say it was all a big joke; he would be angry, but my God, he'd be pleased. Just then the door opened with two police officers.

"What's going on? Am I going home now?"

"Afraid not, son; looks like you're on your way to Durham nick, while you're there, you be on what we call 'Remand' until all the evidence is ready to be heard in front of the judge and a trial be had. We've got your belongings, son; now come on let's me having ya." With that, Ron's fate, at least for the next few weeks, had been decided. It would give him time to try and piece what was happening to him and why. Someone or some people wanted him out the way! And for what? Time was something that he was going to have a lot of, so he would put great use to it in one way or another.

Jimmy

"Right, everyone, listen up; with Ron away, I'm the gaffer now in here; you all got that? Anyone steps out a line, then they'll have me to deal with; ya all know what my temper's like, and there's no one to stop me. This club and the others won't run themselves, will they? Now that's all I have to say; now piss off the lot of ya back to work."

The sweat was running down Jimmy's brow; it was hot in the club, and he'd just made his presence known. He was basking in the glory of being the number one. He'd called the meeting early just as he'd heard the news from Bluewater on Ron's little trip to the nick. Funny thing was Ron was like a brother; after all the years he'd been alongside him, he'd always felt inferior. He had Ron where he wanted him, he had the club, he had Pat, but most importantly, he had the money. He just needed to find the combination for the safe, and he'd be laughing all the way to the bank. He was proud of himself; he took his comb from his pocket and combed his quiff. He glanced at himself in the glass door and smiled. He was the boss now, and everyone will know that soon enough. All he needed was the safe combination, and he would be long gone with the secret stash that Ron had cut him out on over the last four years.

Teddy

"Look, Guv, Are you sure 'bout Bluewater? I keep going over and over in my head about that night, and well, he was first on the scene, he could have been part of it all; it's just we need the evidence, and I think you're gonna have to tell me a lot more about this surveillance you've done on him and bring me into the picture." The Guv hesitated; after all, this was top secret, but he could trust Cartwright. He'd worked with him for years, and well quite frankly, he was the person he wanted to fill his shoes when he takes retirement in the coming months. He paused, deep in thought. It seemed like a good ten minutes before he spoke, and when he did, Teddy would be left open mouthed, that's for sure.

"Well, Teddy, it's like this. A month or so after Bluewater was transferred to us, I was having lunch with a friend down on Boulevard Street. Actually, it was Zanetti's, an exquisite Italian, very, very nice, and well, I glanced out the window and I saw Bluewater with Jimmy Jenkins. They looked very cosy, and it defiantly wasn't anything to do with work. They came in and ordered two Jack Daniels and coke and sat in the booth just behind me. I overheard Bluewater giving Jimmy the heads up on the upcoming raid on the club, and they spoke about gun smuggling also. I heard Bluewater give Jimmy a contact again of another police officer where he could get just the gun he was looking for without a trace back to Ron or himself. They mentioned a Hit and Run and laughed about how easy it would be to get away with it and frame Ron. They also mentioned a huge amount of money that was within their grasp, with Ron out of the way. Look, I'm being honest with you here, and all I want you to do, Teddy, is make sure you're first on the scene at the raid on Ron's place tomorrow. We don't know who else Bluewater is working for or with; there's a lot at stake here. Teddy, without evidence, we won't be able to pin anything on him."

Teddy sighed. "Look, Guv, with all due respect from the way I look at, it is you overheard some dodgy dealings, and now it's happened, and you didn't report it? It doesn't look good, does it? Bluewater should have been reported long ago, so why wasn't he?"

"I couldn't have; it would have jeopardised the whole raid we had planned, and I had orders from above that was not an option; doing it this way I get the evidence to put him, Ron and Jimmy away! For good."

"Agreed, but sir, it goes against the book; he's bent!"

"He's only bent when we have the evidence to say otherwise; now, get the lads rounded up and get the plan of action for tomorrow's raid. We want to be a nice surprise not a one waiting to happen. Bluewater told Jimmy 7 p.m.; well, guess what is 2 a.m. We can make him squirm; I've told Bluewater he's needed at the station front desk tomorrow night, so he's out of the picture. Go and get the troops rounded up…we want a good tomorrow."

"Will do, boss. I won't let you down."

The door slammed with the wind behind the Guv and Teddy jumped. It was going to be a long night indeed…

Jimmy

Jimmy knew he had to act fast; he didn't know the code for the safe and only Ron knew that but…time he didn't have. He was in it up to his neck, he'd betrayed the one person whom he had loved more than life itself, his brother Ron; also the love of his life, Pat. Poor cow didn't have a clue what the plan was once Jimmy had his cut. He was leaving her; he'd outgrown her. He was going to trade her in for someone well more exotic. Get himself a new set of wheels and a one-way ticket out of here, never to return again. He needed that code; the more Jimmy thought about it, the more agitated he was becoming. He'd already lied to Bluewater and gave him a false set of numbers, and he was dead if he didn't find the real code. He remembered the locked desk drawer that he was never allowed to go near…Right, I'm breaking in. He picked a small hacksaw from the set of tools hid in a shaft under the floorboards (meant for torture that they used from time to time). It took him nineteen minutes exactly, and he wasn't disappointed; bingo! Ron's diary along with the codes to both the safe and the gun container. How could he have been so stupid to write them down like that; so easy and all. He laughed greedily; he was now thinking of the money, and Ron rotting in prison for a crime he didn't commit. Jimmy poured himself a brandy and rose his glass.

"To you, Ron Curry, for giving me your million." He knocked his brandy back and threw the glass off a self-portrait off Ron that was hanging above the desk.

He glanced at the clock, shit! It's 7, best get my arse downstairs, ready for this raid. He combed his hair back, lit a cigar and placed the paper with the codes in his back pocket.

"OK, let's do this!"

The club was heaving; with the bad weather outside, they were even busier than usual. Jimmy stepped outside for some air, hoping to catch a glimpse of the cop cars ready for the raid. The rain was torrential; he couldn't see two feet in front of him, never mind police cars. He stumped the cigar out and turned back to walk inside the club.

"Oi, Jimmy, over here; it's me, Bluewater."

Jimmy walked towards where the voice was coming from; he hesitated for a second. He couldn't be certain it was him, but it was too late. Jimmy was gagged and bound and thrown into the back of a waiting car. He felt a fist hit him just below the eye, and then blackness. He was unconscious…

"I've got the codes, boss; don't worry about Jimmy, he's out cold."

"Good work, I like it within the hour deadline swell; you are something else. Keep it warm for me, son; I'll be there in ten."

Bluewater smiled; he didn't really want to hurt Jimmy, and after all, he was instructed to do it. It was only a temporary measure like he would snap back out of it and be none the wiser. They would be in and out in a flash with the money in tow. He rubbed his hands gleefully; it was all going to plan.

Teddy

"You heard, sir, I'm going in now; we've been told Bluewater's gone home sick according to the custody Sarg, and my gut feeling is he could be on his way over to the club. There's no need to send the other boys in just yet we don't want to cause any alarm. I'll give you a bell when all is clear. I've told the boys to wait for the nod, sir."

"You've made yourself quite clear; now get yourself over there. I shall be awaiting a report on my desk for eleven a.m. sharp."

"Thanks, sir; on my way."

Teddy's journey to the club was a complete blur; in all the haze and chaos with the rain and how busy the streets were, he almost failed to spot Bluewater's car. He pulled into the back street, got out and climbed into the front seat of the car.

"Well, Where's the code?"

"Here, it was in his back pocket. I'll wait here on the watch you get yourself up, here there's the key for the office."

"Thanks; not be long then."

Making his way up the back stairs behind the club, Teddy started to wonder how it all went wrong for him; why he got involved in the smuggling. He reminded himself of the real reason his wife and daughters. He lived on a pitiful salary and had waited and waited of promotion. Teddy figured that this set up with Ron, Trev, Bluewater and Jimmy was a no brainer. It would give him the respect of any police officer and his name would be in lights as the one who cracked RON CURRY. If Nancy finds out it would destroy her; she certainly wouldn't stay with him, but it was the desire to be noticed and recognised that made him do it, and when Bluewater joined the force six months ago, he knew he was bent. He'd heard all about him and his back handers. It seemed like the perfect situation.

He turned the key in the lock and stepped inside, now where would he keep his safe. He locked the door behind him and checked his watch; he didn't have long; he needed to be quick. He looked at the wall that was splattered with remnants of brandy and glass. He walked towards it and picked the glass up from the carpet that was now stained and sticky. He was about to replace the glass on the desk when his head knocked the portrait on his way up and fell to the floor. teddy looked up.

"Surprise, Surprise! Look what we have here." Taking out the combination, he imputed the code, and with one click, the safe was opened. Teddy gasped; there was more than a million quid, more like two, but Teddy had to act fast. He decided he would take the lot bar a few ton, that way when Jimmy comes to and gets to the safe, he'll think Ron's hid the money somewhere else. He stuffed his briefcase and left by the stairs he entered. He walked calmly to the car and opened the passenger side.

"Ok, here's the deal. I give you a few thousand, and we forget about all this? You with me?"

"Ah, I'm with ya, and it be more than a few thousand, I want five hundred thousand like that was the deal."

"Look, Ron didn't have that much; looks like we've been played. We're lucky if there ten in total here." Teddy looked into Bluewater's eyes; after all, he was a copper, and they both had a copper's snout for liars. He wondered whether he would be able to see straight through him.

"Look, I'll take it; better than not, Teddy. Look, I'm gonna go travelling, Teddy, and quit the force for a bit. I don't think I could ever have done it without you and your plan, and boy, what a plan it was! I'll be seeing ya, Teddy, don't worry about this one. I'll dump him two miles up the road."

With that, Teddy gave him his cut a nod and stepped out into the night. It was a dark and wet night, but by God, was it the best night of his life…

Jimmy's body was aching. He'd been dumped not far from the club; he'd hit the ground like a ton of bricks. He picked himself up and dusted himself down. Battered and bruised, he stared up at the sky; he'd heard every word between Teddy and Bluewater. He shouted out loud:

"I'M COMING FOR YOU CARTWRIGHT, YOU GOT MY MONEY, AND THAT BELONGS TO ME!"

CPSIA information can be obtained
at www.ICGtesting.com
Printed in the USA
BVHW031006300422
635802BV00016B/684